FJ

24 Hour Telephone Renewals 0845 071 434
HARINGEY
THIS BO...

# This book

# belongs to

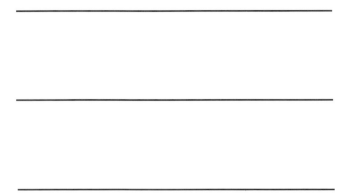

_____

_____

_____

for Rae, Rowan,
Michelle & Alvin.
and a
special Thankyou
to Pauliina for the idea.

First published in
2003 in Great Britain by
Gullane Children's Books
This book & CD edition published in 2006
by Gullane Children's Books
an imprint of Pinwheel Ltd, Winchester House
259-269, Old Marylebone Road
London NW1 5XJ

1 2 3 4 5 6 7 8 9 10
Illustrations © Jane Cabrera 2003
The right of Jane Cabrera to be identified as
the illustrator of this work has been asserted
by her in accordance with the Copyright
Designs, and Patents Act, 1988.

A CIP record for
this title is available
from the British Library
ISBN-13: 978-1-86233-639-1
ISBN-10: 1-86233-639-3

Printed and bound in China

If you're happy and you know it,
NOD your head
If you're happy and you know it,
NOD your head
If you're happy and you know it,
And you really want to show it

If you're happy and you know it,
NOD YOUR HEAD!

If you're happy and you know it,
   ROAR out loud
If you're happy and you know it,
   ROAR out loud
If you're happy and you know it,
And you really want to show it

If you're happy and you know it,

ROAR
OUT LOUD!

If you're happy and you know it,
SPIN AROUND
If you're happy and you know it,
SPIN AROUND
If you're happy and you know it,
And you really want to show it

If you're happy
and you know it,
SPIN AROUND!

H.P.L.

If you're happy and you know it, **FLAP** your arms
If you're happy and you know it, **FLAP** your arms
If you're happy and you know it,

And you really want to show it
If you're happy and you know it,
FLAP YOUR ARMS!

If you're happy and you know it,
   say SQUEAK SQUEAK
If you're happy and you know it,
   say SQUEAK SQUEAK
If you're happy and you know it,
And you really want to show it

If you're happy and you know it, say SQUEAK SQUEAK!

If you're happy and you know it, JUMP ABOUT
If you're happy and you know it, JUMP ABOUT
If you're happy and you know it,
And you really want to show it

If you're happy and you know it,
JUMP ABOUT!

**If you're happy and you know it . . .**

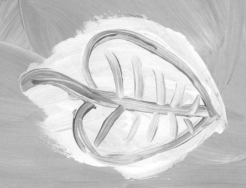

**CLAP YOUR HANDS!**

**ROAR OUT LOUD!**

**SPIN AROUND!**

**SAY SQUEAK SQUEAK!**

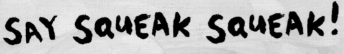

**JUMP ABOUT!**

STAMP YOUR FEET!

NOD YOUR HEAD!

GO KISS KISS!

FLAP YOUR ARMS!

If you're happy and you know it,
And you really want to show it
If you're happy and you know it,

SHOUT...

# Other Gullane Children's Books
# illustrated by Jane Cabrera

## Old Mother Hubbard
### JANE CABRERA
A well-loved traditional nursery rhyme about
Old Mother Hubbard and her hungry dog
who just wants his dinner.

## Eggday
### JOYCE DUNBAR • JANE CABRERA
Dora the duck decides to hold a best egg competition,
but will Pogson the pig, Humphrey the horse
and Gideon the goat stand a chance?

## Over in the Meadow
### JANE CABRERA
Turtles dig, lizards bask, bees buzz and
ratties gnaw in this vibrantly illustrated,
charming counting rhyme.

## Mummy, Carry Me Please!
### JANE CABRERA
All the animals need their mummys to
carry them – very carefully! But each animal is
carried differently. How does your mummy carry you?

GULLANE
CHILDREN'S BOOKS